D0604705

Swim Bark Run

Brian & Pamela Boyle

illustrated by Beth Hughes

Sky Pony Press
New York

To Clara,
Always follow your heart
and dream big.
　　　　—B.B. & P.B.

For Rudy and Sally
　　　　—B.H.

Sky Pony Press books may be purchased at special discounts for sales promotion, corporate gifts, fund-raising, or educational purposes. Special editions can also be created to specifications. For details, contact the Special Sales Department, Sky Pony Press, 307 West 36th Street, 11th Floor, New York, NY 10018 or info@skyhorsepublishing.com.

Sky Pony® is a registered trademark of Skyhorse Publishing, Inc.®, a Delaware corporation.

Visit our website at www.skyponypress.com.

10 9 8 7 6 5 4 3 2 1

Manufactured in China, February 2018. This product conforms to CPSIA 2008

Library of Congress Cataloging-in-Publication Data
Names: Boyle, Brian, 1986- author. | Boyle, Pamela (Nurse), author. | Hughes, Beth, illustrator.
Title: Swim bark run / Brian and Pamela Boyle ; Illustrated by Beth Hughes.
Description: New York : Sky Pony Press, [2018] | Summary: Daisy the bulldog enjoys watching triathlons with her owners so she persuades her friends to hold a triathlon for dogs and, by encouraging each other, they all finish.
| Identifiers: LCCN 2017054930 (print) | LCCN 2018001528 (ebook) | ISBN 9781510726994 (eb) | ISBN 9781510726963 (print : alk. paper) | ISBN 9781510726994 (ebook)
Subjects: | CYAC: Triathlon--Fiction. | Dogs--Fiction. | Teamwork--Fiction. | Determination (Personality trait)--Fiction.
Classification: LCC PZ7.1.B698 (ebook) | LCC PZ7.1.B698 Sw 2018 (print) | DDC [E]--dc23
LC record available at https://lccn.loc.gov/2017054930

Print ISBN: 978-1-5107-2696-3
EBook ISBN: 978-1-5107-2699-4

Cover illustration by Beth Hughes
Cover design by Kate Gartner

Daisy is a little bulldog who loves new adventures.
On cold, rainy days, she imagines exploring the
world warm inside her house.

But when it's nice outside, she likes to swim,
bark, and run in the sun.

Daisy loves when her owners, Brian and Pam, take her to triathlons, races where people swim, ride their bikes, and then run. She likes to sit next to the race course and cheer for Brian as he competes.

One afternoon, lying in the grass, Daisy thought it would be fun to be in a triathlon, too. She couldn't wait to tell all her doggy friends about her new idea.

"That sounds like a lot of fun," said Rascal the Dachshund,
"but what is a triathlon, anyway?"
"How are we going to ride bikes?" asked Atticus the Corgi.

Daisy and her friends had a plan, but there was still a lot of work to do. They decided Rascal would be in charge of creating the race course for his friends. He was now the official race director.

The race would take place at their favorite park.
They'd swim across the small pond.

Then, they would skateboard on the sidewalk that went halfway around the pond. Finally, they would run on the wooded trail straight to the finish line.

Training was tough. The friends swam across the pond.

They practiced skateboarding in a line.

They ran up and down the hills.

They practiced for weeks, and before they knew it, race day was here. As they lined up at the starting line, Rascal chanted into the megaphone,

"Swim, bark, run! Everyone have fun!"

Hobie took an early lead during the swim. Daisy and Atticus did their best to keep up. They liked doggy paddling across the pond and smiled as they splished and splashed to the shore.

Daisy realized that Atticus was having trouble keeping up, so she waited patiently until he reached the shore.
They began the next stage of the race together.
As Daisy and Atticus sped around the pond on their skateboards,

the wind rushed over their fur. Daisy was a very good skateboarder, but Atticus noticed she wasn't going as fast as she could.

"Go faster, Daisy!" Atticus called.
"Try to catch up with Hobie."

"Are you sure?" she asked
Atticus smiled and nodded, and
Daisy zipped off on Hobie's tail.

In no time at all, Daisy had not only caught up to Hobie, but she'd passed him.

ZOOM!

She was racing up and down the hills, bolting around the course's curves.

She was in the lead!

Daisy finished the skateboard section ahead of Hobie and Atticus, and started running fast down the trail. But soon she realized she'd used up too much energy on her skateboard.

Hobie sprinted ahead of her. "Go Hobie, go! she cheered.

Daisy was running slower and slower. Soon Atticus caught up to her.
"You're doing great," he called.
"Thanks, Atticus. You run ahead, I'll be fine."
He stayed by Daisy's side for a few minutes, before running
after Hobie.

Coming around a turn, Daisy looked up at the big hill in front of her, and then sat down on the trail. "I'm tired," she said to herself. "I don't know if I can do this."

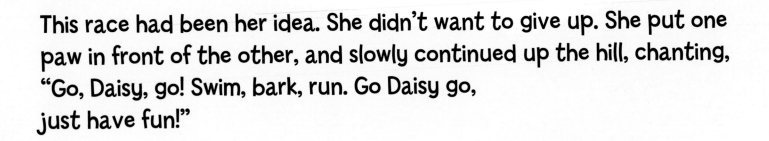

This race had been her idea. She didn't want to give up. She put one paw in front of the other, and slowly continued up the hill, chanting, "Go, Daisy, go! Swim, bark, run. Go Daisy go, just have fun!"

When she made it to the top of the hill, she couldn't believe her eyes. Brian was standing there waving at her!

Daisy had always gone to Brian's races, and now he was at her race.

She felt a new burst of energy and confidence.

"I'll be waiting for you at the finish line, Daisy!" Brian cheered. "You're doing great!"

Daisy ran so fast that all anyone could see were her paw prints left in the dirt. She was determined to finish this race!

She saw the finish line in the distance. Hobie, Brian, and Pam were there calling, "Go, Daisy, go!"

Atticus slowed down so he could finish right by her side. Rascal shouted into his megaphone:

"Swim, bark, run!
Did everyone have fun?" They were all cheering.

After Daisy crossed the finish line, Brian placed a shiny gold medal around her neck. She was so proud.

Together, Daisy and her friends had helped each other to keep going, even when the race got hard, and now they were all winners.